Herbie Jones
and the Birthday Showdown

Herbie Jones
and the Birthday Showdown

by Suzy Kline

illustrated by Carl Cassler

G. P. Putnam's Sons • New York

Acknowledgments

Thank you for inspiring this story:

Jack Schaefer's *Shane*
Jennifer's and Emily's birthday parties
Nonna and Pops
Utz Potato Chip factory tour in Hanover, Pennsylvania
The boy from Minnesota who suggested a new definition of RSVP
The American Cowboy by Harold McCracken
And Rufus, who, as usual, thought of the title
and talked about the story with me.

And special appreciation to my editor,
Anne O'Connell, who helped me write it.

Excerpt from *Shane* by Jack Schaefer. Copyright © 1949,
renewed 1976 by Jack Schaefer. Reprinted by permission
of Houghton Mifflin Co. All rights reserved.

Text copyright © 1993 by Suzy Kline.
Illustrations copyright © 1993 by Carl Cassler.
Interior artwork on pages 35, 74, 76, and 77 by Patrick Collins.
G. P. Putnam's Sons, a division of
The Putnam & Grosset Group, 200 Madison Avenue, New York, NY 10016.
G. P. Putnam's Sons, Reg. U.S. Pat. & Tm. Off.
Published simultaneously in Canada. Printed in the United States of America.
Book designed by Colleen Flis. Text set in Caledonia.
Library of Congress Cataloging-in-Publication Data
Kline, Suzy. Herbie Jones and the birthday showdown / Suzy Kline.   p.   cm.
Summary: When Ray decides to throw a party for his ninth
birthday, in competition with another boy with the same
birthday and more money, he asks his best friend Herbie to
help him find an idea that is new, exciting, and free.
[1. Birthdays—Fiction. 2. Parties—Fiction. 3. Schools—Fiction. 4.
Friendship—Fiction.] I. Title. PZ7.K6797Hfh 1993
[Fic]—dc20 93–3383 CIP AC
ISBN 0-399-22600-1
1   3   5   7   9   10   8   6   4   2
First Impression

For my daughter
Emily Kline,
*who started her high school newspaper
and was its editor for three years.
Thank you for your help with
this manuscript.
I love you.*

Contents

1
Birthday Showdown

Herbie Jones looked outside his classroom window at the bright red and yellow leaves on the maple tree. When a big van pulled up, Herbie watched a clown get out with two dozen balloons.

"Hey, Ray!" he whispered.

Raymond Martin was reading *History of the American Hamburger* for the second time. "What?"

"Look out the window."

Ray did.

Herbie expected Ray to smile and say neato. But he didn't.

"Probably birthday balloons for some lucky kid in kindergarten," Ray groaned. Then he went back to his book.

"Ray," Herbie whispered again. "*Your* birthday is one week from tomorrow. Aren't you getting excited?"

"Nah."

"Why not?"

"John Greenweed's birthday is the same day as mine, remember?"

Herbie nodded. John always had his party on October 8. The past two years Ray had his the day before or the day after.

Herbie knew it was a sore point. This year October 8 was a Saturday.

The last time Ray and John celebrated their birthday on the same day, four people showed up at Ray's party.

Herbie and Ray's three cousins.

Ray never had it on the same day as John's again.

"Maybe you could talk to him about it," Herbie suggested. "You guys should take turns."

"Yeah," Ray said, looking hopeful.

At ten o'clock, Miss Pinkham closed her book. "Boys and girls, next Thursday is Grandparents' Day, and I thought it would be nice for your committees to share what you have learned about the United States in the 1800s."

Herbie beamed. This was the first year he would have a grandparent come. Grandpa Jones was visiting all the way from California for two whole weeks. Herbie's other grandparents lived in Indiana and they just visited during the holidays.

Annabelle Louisa Hodgekiss raised her hand. "My committee is making great progress on women in the 1800s. Did you know Susan B. Anthony, Harriet Tubman, and Florence Nightingale were all born in 1820? Clara Barton was born a year later, in 1821."

"How interesting!" Miss Pinkham said.

"I know something more interesting," Ray replied. "John Greenweed and I were born on the same day *and* the same year."

John held up two fingers for victory.

Annabelle rolled her eyeballs.

"Coincidences are amazing," Miss Pinkham replied. "Any other reports?"

While the class talked, Ray started writing a note to John.

Ten minutes later, the teacher called on Herbie

and Ray. "Have you two decided yet what your project is? Time is running out."

"We know," Herbie said. "It has something to do with the wild West, right, Ray?"

Ray looked up. "Right."

Herbie continued, "Ray and I've been collecting data about western life."

"Oh?" Miss Pinkham seemed impressed with Herbie's use of the word "data." "What sources are you using?"

Herbie smiled. "Videos. Have you ever seen *Shane, Gunfight at the O.K. Corral* or *High Noon*? They're great!"

The teacher folded her arms. "Yes, I have seen them, Herbie, but I hope you're planning on doing some reading, too."

"We are. We're halfway through *Shane*. My granddad is reading it to us."

Miss Pinkham smiled. "That's great." Then she reached for a book near her desk. "Here's another book about cowboys you can use in class."

"Thanks," Herbie said.

"Okay, boys and girls, get together with your committees."

Herbie moved his chair across the aisle to Ray's. "What are you writing?"

"A note to John. Want to read it?"

Herbie did.

DEAR JOHN,

I tHINK IT WOLD BE NICE IF YOU DID'Nt HAVE YOUR PARtY ON OCtOBER 8 tHIS YAR. THE LASt TWO YARS YOU HAD It ON tHE 8. LEt ME NOW BECAUSE I WANt to StART PLANING MY PARtY AND I WANt A tURN tO HAVE It ON tHE 8.

RAY

P.S. I'LL INVItE YOU tO MY PARtY ON tHE 8.

"Good letter, Ray," Herbie said. He decided not to mention the misspelled words.

Ray looked over at John. He and Phillip were on the floor sketching a train on a big piece of paper. The timing was perfect. Lots of people were out of their seats.

Ray quickly walked over and dropped the folded

13

note in front of John, and then returned to look at the cowboy book with Herbie.

A few minutes later, John stood over Ray's desk. "There's no way I'm moving my party to another day."

"But that's not fair."

"Of course, it's fair. It's my birthday. I can do whatever I want. And so can you."

Ray stood up and stared him in the eye. "John Greenweed, if you want a birthday showdown, you've got one."

John cracked up. "Ol' cowboy Ray! You'll regret this. Remember the last time you challenged me? Everyone came to my birthday except your buddy here, Herbie."

Ray gritted his teeth. "We'll see about that. Next Saturday."

John strolled back to his seat, laughing.

Herbie put his hands on his head. "Ray, are you crazy? You know what kind of a party John gives. The kind that goes places like miniature golfing and roller skating. And he gives loot bags, too. Your dad was laid off last summer. He's only been back to work a few weeks now. You can't afford a flashy party."

"I'm not backing out of this. I have the same right to have a party on my birthday as John."

Herbie shook his head.

He could just picture Ray and John at the O.K. Corral shooting it out. After the gunsmoke settled, it was Ray who was on the ground full of holes.

2
Invitation Disaster

Monday morning before the bell, Herbie watched John and Ray pass out their birthday invitations.

It was just as he thought. They were both inviting the *same* eight people.

Slowly, Herbie opened the two cards on his desk.

One had a picture of a baseball player batting a ball on the cover. The words said: COME TO A GRAND SLAM PARTY!

The other card had a picture of blue skies and puffy clouds. The words said: IN THE HOUR OF YOUR SORROW.

Herbie knew which one was Ray's.

Quickly, he leaned over and whispered, "Ray, what are you doing sending sympathy cards?"

"Sorry about that. I had to give that one to you. There weren't too many birthday ones in the box."

"What box?"

"My mom has had it around the house for a year. I figured if I could save her some money, I might be able to give loot bags this year like John."

Herbie tipped back in his chair. He needed a moment to choose the right words. Calling Ray an air-head probably wouldn't help.

"Ray, that was a box of occasion cards. They're not meant to be invitations. Didn't you read what they said?"

"I never read cards," Ray replied. "I picked out the ones with the neatest pictures and then printed the date and time and place of my birthday on the inside."

Herbie tried to be optimistic. "Okay, maybe it'll work." Then he looked over at Annabelle. She was just taking Ray's invitation out of the envelope.

"A get-well card? Raymond, I'm not sick."

Herbie smiled. "Maybe we can do something about that."

"Herbie Jones! *That's* not funny!" Annabelle snapped. She didn't like it when he teased her.

17

"Nice picture of a dog," Margie said. "I have the exact same card."

Annabelle looked at the cocker spaniel with a thermometer in his mouth and groaned.

" 'Congratulations on your wedding'?" Jose said, holding his card up.

"Look at the pink convertible car on the cover," Margie noted.

Ray gritted his teeth. No one but Margie appreciated the pictures. And no one was reading the inside that explained everything.

"I was just kidding," Ray replied. "Tear up those cards. The *real ones* are coming tomorrow."

Annabelle ripped hers first.

Phillip ripped his second.

John folded his into an airplane and flew it into the garbage. "You can't compete with my party, Ray. We're going to the batting cages and having foot-long hot dogs for lunch. What are you doing? Pin the tail on the donkey?"

Ray walked up to John. He held his head high and his shoulders back. "I am doing what no one has *ever* done at a birthday party at our school."

"What?"

"You'll find out tomorrow."

As soon as Ray got back to his seat, he tugged on Herbie's shirt. "You've got to help me. What can I do that's new, exciting, and doesn't cost any money?"

Herbie put his hand on his forehead like he had a splitting headache. "Come over after school, Ray. We'll work on it."

3

Picking Brains in the Attic

After school that day, Herbie grabbed something to eat and headed on up the stairs to the attic.

Ray trudged behind him.

So did Herbie's dog, Hamburger Head.

When the boys passed the attic window that overlooked the backyard, they could see Grandpa Jones and Mr. Jones making a wooden wheelbarrow in the garage.

"Neato," Herbie said.

Ray didn't say anything. His mind was on his party.

As soon as they walked across the attic floor and into the little room, Ray plopped down on the bed. "What about my birthday? Where can we go and what can we do?"

Herbie set a bag of potato chips on the table. "That *doesn't* cost money."

He and Ray crunched on chips and thought.

Finally, Ray put his arms behind his back. "Can't go to the movies, Burger Paradise, miniature golf, roller skating, or the amusement park."

"Ray," Herbie said. "Maybe you should think about what you *can* do and not what you can't."

"Yeah, you're right."

Herbie walked over to the attic window. It was wide open and the breeze felt good. Herbie could see some dark clouds setting in.

"You know, Ray, I have my birthdays at home and they're a lot of fun. You don't have to *go* anywhere. Remember my last party, when we had a treasure hunt in my backyard?"

Ray nodded. "That last clue was a toughy. How did it go?"

"Clue number five is on something alive."

"Right!" Ray said, sitting up. "It was on Hamburger Head. John Greenweed figured it out and he got the treasure. A coupon for a cheeseburger at Burger Paradise."

Ray fell back on the bed and dreamed.

Herbie shrugged. "Do you want to have a treasure hunt for your party? I'll help write the clues."

Ray shook his head. "I said my party would be something different. Something that no one has done yet at Laurel Woods Elementary School."

"They'd be different clues."

"Forget it, Herbie."

Suddenly a thunderbolt exploded and heavy rain thumped against the house. Just as Herbie closed the window, he saw a car pull up and Olivia get out.

"THANKS!" she called.

Herbie smiled. He thought it was fun when his sister got sopping wet.

When the boys heard footsteps across the attic and a knock at the door, Herbie knew who it was before he opened it.

"Hi, Olive," he said.

Olivia moved a wet clump of hair out of her eyes. "Band practice was cancelled. I'm psyched!"

"I thought you liked band," Herbie said.

"Not since we got our uniforms. Have you seen the hats?"

Ray nodded. "I did at the Labor Day parade. The high school band looked like they had green wastepaper baskets on their heads."

Olivia laughed. "I look six feet tall in mine."

Herbie didn't say anything. He knew height was a sore subject with his sister.

"So, what do you want?" Herbie asked. His sister didn't usually drop by for a chat.

"I wanted to read one of my old Sugar Mountain High books. They're stored up here in that bookcase."

Herbie turned. The top shelf had books perfectly numbered 1 through 85. As he watched his sister select Volume 41, he suddenly wondered if she might be able to help them with their birthday problem. Herbie decided to stall her awhile.

"Eh . . . what's number 41 about?"

Olivia stopped halfway to the door. She liked the question. "Well, let's see. Victoria Ashford and Brittany Fairchild are fighting over Blaine Rutherford III."

"Doesn't anybody have a plain name like Shane?"

"Herbie, a name has to have a little romance to it."

When Olivia said that, Herbie and Ray exchanged looks. The conversation was getting deadly. Herbie knew he had to make a direct hit.

"Can we pick your brain?"

"I hate that expression, Herbie. It's gross."

"Can I?"

"Yes." Then she plopped down on the bed. "What's up?"

"Ray needs to do something on his birthday that's exciting, has never been done before in Laurel Woods, and doesn't cost any money."

Olivia took a handful of potato chips. "You've got to be kidding."

"No. Ray and me thought you could help us think of something."

"Ray and *I!*" Olivia scolded.

Herbie got up and pulled the door wide open. "Grammar interferes with great minds. Good-bye, Olive."

Olivia started to leave, then stopped halfway. "Oh, Herbie, there is *one* thing you could do."

"What?" the boys asked.

"Have a nose-picking party."

"*Yeah!*"

Olivia looked at the boys in disbelief. "I was *kidding!*"

"We're not!" Herbie replied. "Hey, we could play: whoever picks the most boogers wins a prize."

"Herbie Jones, you are *so* disgusting!"

After Olivia stomped out of the room, Herbie and Ray slapped each other five and cracked up.

Then Ray put his chin on his hand. "Let's face it. We're not going to come up with anything."

Herbie tossed Ray the bag of chips. Food always kept his spirits up.

Just as Ray caught the bag, he noticed something boxed in red on the back. "Hey! Look at this!"

Herbie and Ray read the message: VISIT OUR LUTZ POTATO CHIP FACTORY. FREE TOURS MONDAY THROUGH SATURDAY, 10 AM TO 5 PM.

"Where are their factories?" Herbie asked. Then he read the small print: " 'Fort Worth, Texas; Des Moines, Iowa; Trenton, New Jersey; and our newest plant in Waterbury, Connecticut.' "

"WATERBURY!" the boys shouted.

"That's only thirty minutes away!" Ray said. "We bought our washing machine there."

Herbie slapped his buddy five. "No one at school has had a birthday party at a *potato chip factory*."

Ray held up the bag. "Boy, did I come up with a biggie!"

"A *free* biggie!" Herbie replied.

"An exciting biggie!" Ray added. "I bet we even get *free* samples. I won't have to bug Mom about loot bags! Herbie, this is going to be the best party of my life!"

"YAHOO!" the boys shouted.

Then they finished the chips and popped the bag.

Blam!

4
Stormy Night

That night Herbie couldn't sleep.

Every time the thunder rumbled, he pulled the covers over his head. What if the maple tree just outside his window cracked in two?

And where was Hamburger Head?

Herbie peeked out of the covers and looked at the clock. It was 10:30. Maybe his dad hadn't left yet for his nightshift job.

Herbie jumped out of bed and raced across the attic. As soon as he got to the stairwell, he could see Hamburger Head at the bottom of the steps. He wanted out, too.

Quickly Herbie opened the attic door, dashed across the hallway, and opened the kitchen door.

"Dad!" he shouted. "Good . . . to see you."

Mr. Jones was sipping coffee and eating some oatmeal cookies.

"Hi, son. You still up?"

"Yeah." Herbie sat down next to his dad at the kitchen table.

"The storm bother you?"

"A little. Want to talk for a while?"

Mr. Jones smiled at his son. "Sure. I haven't seen you much the last few days. What's going on?"

Herbie thought for a moment. "Showdowns. What do you think of them?"

Mr. Jones laughed. "Showdowns? You mean the kind the cowboys had?"

"Yeah."

"Well, I think it's far better to settle things with a compromise than a shootout."

"What do you mean, compromise?"

"Talk things over. Each person gives up a little so they can both do at least part of what they set out to do."

Herbie liked that.

Just then Grandpa Jones came into the kitchen. Herbie thought his striped pajamas were neat. He looked like he had just escaped from prison.

"Didn't mean to eavesdrop, but I agree with your dad, Herbie. Compromisin' is much better than showdowns."

Herbie watched his grandpa pour himself some prune juice. "Your dad and I wanted to build something. He wanted to make a ladder. I wanted to make a wheelbarrow. So we talked it over and decided to make a wheelbarrow."

"How's that a compromise?" Herbie asked. He liked using the new word.

Mr. Jones got up from the table. "Yeah, Pops, explain that one, huh?"

"Well, we're still thinking about makin' a ladder."

Herbie nodded.

Mr. Jones laughed. "He's just plain stubborn, Herbie. Come here, cowboy, and give me a hug."

Herbie threw his arms around his dad.

Then he watched him take a lunch out of the refrigerator, grab his jacket and coffee thermos, and leave for the airplane factory in the black stormy night.

"YOU WORK HARD, DAD. LIKE SHANE!"

Mr. Jones didn't hear Herbie, but his granddad did.

"Come on, partner, I'll walk you upstairs, and read to you for a while."

"Thanks, Grandpa. Would you read me that part again where Shane chops down the big tree stump?"

"Sure."

5
Martin House of Cards

Herbie didn't meet Raymond on the corner the next day. He went ten minutes early and directly to Ray's house. He wanted to make sure Ray had okayed things with his mother. Was she willing to drive to Waterbury? And what about the invitations? Herbie had to make sure Ray *wasn't* using occasion cards again.

Herbie walked across Ray's tall lawn. The Martins didn't mow very often. As soon as he rang the bell, he heard Shadow bark.

Mrs. Martin opened the door. As usual, she had some paint on her shirt. Herbie thought it was neat that she was an artist.

"Good morning, Herbie! Come on in. Ray's in the pantry."

31

"The pantry?"

Herbie petted Shadow and then walked through the dark living room. The Martins never opened their curtains. The coffee table had an old box of pizza on it and there were newspapers all over the floor.

Herbie followed Mrs. Martin into the pantry.

"Don't laugh!" Ray scolded.

Herbie took a step back. Raymond was sitting in a chair with a shirt and tie on, his hair combed, and his face tilted slightly to the left.

The easel next to him had a picture that looked just like Raymond although it was still unfinished.

"Wow! That's terrific, Mrs. Martin."

"Thanks, Herbie. It's Ray's portrait at nine years. Kind of a birthday present."

"Boring birthday present," Ray complained. "Can I change now?"

"Two more minutes. I want to fill in your left eyebrow."

Ray groaned, then he looked up at Herbie. "How come you're early today?"

Herbie decided to come right out in the open. He wanted to make sure Ray's mother knew about

everything. "You have your invitations for your potato chip birthday party Saturday?"

"Yup."

Herbie breathed easier.

"Mom helped me make them. Go ahead and open yours. They're in the refrigerator."

Herbie smiled. He knew that's where the Martins kept important things. Herbie spotted the stack next to the jar of pickled beet slices. His was on top.

Herbie opened the envelope. A white card was folded in half and said:

You Are Invited to the First Potato Chip Birthday Party!

Herbie looked at the potato chip on the front. "Did you paint this? It looks just like a chip."

"Mom did. She did the lettering, too."

Herbie read the inside of the card.

Who: Raymond Martin's
9th Birthday
What: Tour Lutz Potato
Chip Factory
When: Saturday 2:00~5:00
(Tour is at 3:00)

R.S.V.P

The times were almost perfect! Herbie remembered John's invitation said 11:00 to 3:00. All he had to do was get John to compromise one hour and everyone could go to *both* birthdays that day.

"All right!" Herbie said. Then he turned the card over. "Hmmmm . . . I see the part you did, Ray."

Ray held up two fingers.

Down at the bottom was a Viking ship and the words MARTIN HOUSE OF CARDS.

"So," Herbie asked as he tucked the card in his back jeans pocket, "you know what RSVP means?"

"Sure I do," Ray said. "It's *not* Remove Shoes Very Promptly. It means Really Scary Vampire Party."

Mrs. Martin shook her head when the boys fell to the floor, laughing. "Okay, you sillies," she said. "If all the children can come, Ray's father will bring his truck and I'll drive the car."

Herbie stood up.

Things weren't funny anymore. Ray's party was for real. He had planned it with his mom.

Suddenly a big black cloud of doom floated inside Herbie's head.

What if John wouldn't compromise and most of the kids still went to John's party?

6

Compromise?

That Tuesday in class, before the bell, Ray passed out his birthday invitations.

"Who painted the potato chip?" Annabelle asked.

"Me," Ray beamed. "I used Mom's paints."

Herbie shot Ray a look.

"Exciting!" Margie replied. "Ray's party is going to tour that new Lutz Potato Chip plant!"

"I bet you get free samples," Jose said.

"You do," Ray said, making his eyebrows go up and down.

"I drove by that place," Phillip said. "Man, it smelled like rotten potatoes. P.U. Aaaaaauugh! Glarggg . . . blaugh." Phillip liked to make silly noises.

John cracked up. "Too bad most of us will miss Ray's smelly party. We'll be having too much fun at mine."

Ray held up a fist.

That was Herbie's cue. "Hey, John," he whispered. "Can I talk to you for a minute by the globes?"

"Sure. I haven't gotten your RSVP yet. See my list?"

Herbie looked. There were four names: Phillip, Annabelle, Sarah, and John.

"John who?" Herbie asked.

"Me."

So, Herbie thought, he had three coming. With luck, Ray would get three, too.

"What do you want?" John asked as he spinned the globe. "I know you're going to Ray's party."

Suddenly Herbie got an inspiration. "Yeah, but . . . I want to come to yours, too."

"You do?"

"I look forward to going to your parties, John. They're neat." Herbie knew a little buttering up wouldn't hurt.

John beamed.

"I was just wondering if you might consider compromising a little."

John stopped smiling. "What do you mean . . . compromise?"

"I think it would be great if everyone could go to both parties this year on October eighth."

"Impossible. The times are wrong."

"Wait a minute, John. How 'bout you shortening your party just one hour? Make it eleven to two instead of eleven to three. That way everyone could go to both. And both parties would be three hours."

"WHAT? I have my party planned down to the minute. It might even go later than three." John spun the globe again, keeping his finger still. When it stopped, his finger landed in the middle of the Pacific Ocean.

"I don't like being rushed. The times for my party *stay*."

Herbie didn't like John's tone of voice when he said "stay." He was acting tough like Stark Wilson in *Shane*. That was the guy who had a showdown with Ernie in the saloon. Stark Wilson won.

"Well, I want you to know, John, that I am going to your birthday party . . ."

"Great, Herbie, I'll add you to the list!"

"However," Herbie added, "I'll be leaving an hour early so I can go to Ray's, too. Who knows, maybe a group of people will follow me."

John snarled as Herbie took his turn spinning the globe, keeping his finger still and waiting for the whirl to stop. "Aha! Timbuktu, my favorite place."

John stomped his foot as Herbie went back to his seat.

Ray was frowning when he saw Herbie return. "Annabelle just told me she's going to John's party. She also said potato chips have too many grams of fat in them. And that they are not a wholesome, nutritious snack."

Herbie recognized the words "wholesome, nutritious snack." His mother said it a lot.

"So who cares if Annabelle comes or not?" Herbie groaned.

"I do," Ray replied. "She gives the best presents."

Herbie nodded. Ray was right.

When the bell rang and Miss Pinkham had the class work on their projects for Grandparents' Day, Herbie was relieved. The whole birthday business was getting to Herbie. He needed a break from it.

"Why don't we list the things we know about cowboys," Herbie suggested.

Ray took out a piece of paper. "Let's see, I'm coming, you're coming, Margie is a maybe, and so is Sarah. Jose said he'd let me know tomorrow."

"RAY!" Herbie said. "We're supposed to make a display of cowboy life and give a presentation for Thursday. Aren't your grandparents coming?"

"Just Grandma Martin."

"Well, don't you want to make a good presentation for Grandma Martin?"

"Now that I think of it, yeah! She usually puts five dollars in a birthday card, but this year, if I do a great presentation, she might throw in a few extra bucks."

Herbie socked his buddy in the arm. "Okay. Let's start listing facts. Then maybe we could think of a skit."

Ray perked up. "Yeah, a showdown! I get to fill you full of lead."

"Oh yeah?" Herbie said. He put his nose next to Ray's and tried to look as fierce as he could. "You've got a reservation at Boot Hill."

"Is that a restaurant?" Ray asked.

"No," Herbie said. "It's a cemetery for cowboys who die with their boots on."

Annabelle raised her eyebrows as she peeked over her book. She was going to have to speak with the boys about an important matter.

After school.

7
Cowgirls and Annabelle

Tuesday at 3:15, Herbie and Ray were reading about cowboys in the school library. Mrs. Reed, the school librarian, was helping some of Herbie's classmates get more books about the 1800s.

Herbie liked the pencils in her hair. They had rattlesnake erasers.

Annabelle walked over to the boys. "I overheard you in class today. Doing a skit about the wild West?"

"Yup," Ray answered, "and you'll love it so much, you'll change your mind and come to my potato chip birthday party."

Annabelle laughed. Then she lowered her eyebrows. "I suppose your skit is going to be a typical western-style shoot 'em up, blow 'em out, and fill 'em full of lead skit."

Just as Ray started to say yes, Herbie covered Ray's mouth.

"As a matter of fact," Herbie said, "most cowboys didn't wear guns. They kept them hanging up high somewhere."

"Or under their bunk like Shane," Ray added. He liked knowing something that Annabelle didn't.

Annabelle raised her eyebrows. "Really? Well, I would never have a gun *anywhere* in my house."

"Me either," Herbie agreed. Then he opened his book to a certain page. "See, it says here that the most important thing to a cowboy was his word. Whenever he gave his handshake, that sealed the deal."

"Some were honest, I suppose," Annabelle replied. "But all they cared about was making money."

"Hold on!" Herbie said. "See this picture? The cowboy is risking his life to save a lost calf. He cared about the animals and land, too."

Annabelle glanced at Herbie's book. "I bet

women are not mentioned. Your presentation will just be about men. There *were* women in the West, too, you know. Susan B. Anthony lectured there about women's rights."

Herbie grinned. "Yup, and I know the names of three cowgirls—Cattle Kate, Belle Starr, and Calamity Jane." Herbie decided not to tell Annabelle that the first two were cattle and horse thieves and the third chewed tobacco.

Annabelle made a small smile and then returned to her seat.

Herbie and Ray slapped each other five.

Then Herbie got a sudden thought.

So *now* what do we do for a skit?

8
Snap, Crackle, and Chew

That night after dinner, the phone rang so Herbie picked it up. He knew the voice.

"Hey, Ray. Got an idea for our skit?"

"No. I need an idea for a treat."

"A treat?"

"I bumped into John at the grocery store about ten minutes ago. I had to pick up some milk for dinner."

"Yeah." Herbie was waiting for Ray to get to the point.

"And John was near the freezers with his mom. He was buying two dozen Eskimo Pies. He's handing them out in class Friday for his birthday treat."

"I'll look forward to that," Herbie said. Then he pictured the rich chocolate bar with creamy vanilla ice cream in the middle. His family never bought them because they were too expensive. When they did get ice cream, it was always the store brand.

"Herbie!"

"What?" His picture of the Eskimo Pie was fading.

"What do I pass out for a treat?"

"You can figure it out, Ray. It's not that important."

"It *is* important. I have two people coming to my party for sure. You and me. Everyone else is a maybe."

Herbie didn't say anything. He knew it was true. This was what he was afraid of all along.

"So," Ray continued, "I was thinking I could beat John to the draw."

Herbie smiled. The West was getting to Ray.

"Look, if I pass out my treats early, people will start thinking about *my* birthday. Thursday is Grandparents' Day, so that's shot. It's got to be tomorrow. Wednesday."

"Okay, Ray, what do you want to do?"

"I want you to come over and help me bake something."

"Bake?" Herbie thought about it. He and Ray had never baked anything before.

"Hey, why not?"

When Herbie got to Ray's house, Ray was standing at the open door chewing a wad of gum.

Herbie could smell it was grape. "Have another piece?"

Ray reached into his pocket and unwrapped half a stick. "You're in luck!"

Herbie popped it into the front of his mouth and pretended it was chewing tobacco.

As the boys walked through the dark living room into the kitchen, they heard Mr. Martin snoring on the couch. The newspaper was over his chest. Herbie knew why Mr. Martin was tired. He was a janitor and had to sweep 25 classrooms a day.

Mrs. Martin was busy dabbling with Ray's portrait in the pantry. She didn't even come out into the kitchen. She just called, "Hi, Herbie!"

"Hi, Mrs. Martin. So, Ray, what are we making?"

"Well, I looked around the cupboards and found

a recipe on the back of a cereal box. Have you ever made Rice Krispies Treats?"

Herbie shook his head.

"The best part is you don't even have to turn the oven on. Which is good, because ours isn't working. Just the burners."

Herbie rolled his eyeballs.

Ray got a big pot out of the cupboard. The outside was solid black but it was clean on the inside. "Now the back of the box says we melt one-quarter of a cup of margarine."

Herbie took a stick from the refrigerator. "Look, Ray, it has the measurements right on the paper. Half a stick of margarine is one-quarter of a cup."

Ray cut it in half and dropped it in the pot. Then he turned the burner on, carefully like his mother taught him to when he made soup. " 'Add forty marshmallows,' " Ray read.

"That's the same as the whole bag," Herbie said. "It says so."

"You mean we can't even have one apiece?" Ray moaned.

"Sure," Herbie replied. "We can make Rice

Krispies Treats with thirty-eight marshmallows. Here, have one."

The boys bit into the soft, sweet marshmallows and said, "Mmmmm."

" 'Stir until' . . . what's that word, Herbie?"

" '*Completely* melted.' "

The boys took turns stirring.

"This is a cinch!" Ray said.

Herbie agreed.

"Now it says to add the Rice Krispies."

The boys poured the cereal into the pot. Some spilled onto the table and the floor, but the boys didn't notice. "Man," Herbie said, "this stuff is gooey!"

"Neat, huh? Let's use our hands."

"Wash 'em first," Herbie said.

The boys did, under the kitchen spigot.

Then they mooshed the cereal and marshmallow goo together. "Ooooooooh! Neato!" Herbie said.

"Hear it snap and crackle?" Ray added.

The boys laughed as they squished the mixture through their fingers.

Ray got a glass dish and smeared butter on it

with his fingers. "Okay, let's smash this stuff in here."

Herbie helped.

"Ta dah!" the boys said.

"A work of art, Mom," Ray called. "Come and see."

Mrs. Martin peeked around the corner. She had paint on her face. "Looks great, boys!"

When Herbie walked in the house that night, he bragged about his cooking adventure to his sister.

"I don't believe it," Olivia replied. "You and Ray *actually* followed directions step by step in that recipe?"

"Yup. In fact, we're planning to be cowboy cooks for our skit Thursday in class."

"I'm impressed," Olivia said. Then she blew a pink bubble.

Suddenly Herbie's face turned pink.

What had happened to his grape gum?

9
The Purple Treat

Wednesday afternoon, Annabelle's committee was busy making dioramas. Jose's committee was constructing a huge lighthouse out of Tinkertoys. John and Phillip were adding paint to the Santa Fe train.

"Everyone is working so hard," Miss Pinkham said as she visited each group. "I'm sure the grandparents will love the displays."

Herbie eyed Ray's birthday treats on the back table and crossed his fingers. The 23 individually wrapped treats sat on a plate covered with cellophane. Herbie didn't have the heart to tell Ray. He just said a silent prayer that *he* would be the one to get the treat with the chewy purple center.

Meanwhile Miss Pinkham stopped by Herbie's

and Ray's desks. Herbie was printing the rules that cooks had at the cow camp, while Ray was making a chuckwagon out of a shoebox and white handkerchief. Herbie had brought little pots and pans from Olivia's old dollhouse in the attic to hang from the wagon.

"Everyone did their own dishes out West," Herbie said, "or you didn't eat."

Miss Pinkham smiled. "That's a great rule." Then she announced, "It's time for a birthday break!"

The class cheered.

Except Herbie.

He slowly sank down in his seat.

"Let's sing 'Happy Birthday' to Raymond first," Miss Pinkham said.

Raymond got his plate of treats and stood in front of the room, beaming. Herbie could tell Ray loved the attention.

He could also tell Ray's strategy was working. The excitement over the treats stimulated a conversation between Margie and Sarah. They were talking about how they could leave John's party early so they could go to Ray's.

When the class started singing the happy birth-day song, Herbie started thinking. He had goofed up something that was important to Ray, and he hadn't even told him.

By the time everyone was singing the second verse—"How old are you now?"—Herbie's con-science really bothered him.

"Would you like to choose a helper?" Miss Pink-ham asked Ray.

Everyone looked at Herbie. They knew Ray would pick him.

"Herbie," Ray said. "He's the best friend any-body could have. He also helped me make these treats."

Herbie felt two inches tall. He was *not* the best friend anybody could have. He really failed Ray this time.

Quickly he walked up to the front of the room. "Ray," he whispered, "I *have* to tell you some-thing."

"What?"

"You know that grape gum you gave me last night?"

"Yeah."

"I think it . . . dropped into one of the . . ."

"TREATS?"

Herbie nodded as Ray handed him the plate.

Ray shook his head. "Nah, it probably just dropped on the floor and got stuck to someone's shoe."

Herbie and Ray immediately lifted up their sneakers and checked the soles. Herbie's left shoe had a thumbtack. Ray's right one had some dried dog doo.

No gum.

"Don't worry about it," Ray said.

Herbie watched Ray place the first treat on Phillip's desk. The theme song from the old TV show "Dragnet" went through Herbie's head.

"Dun da dun dun," he hummed.

Ray put another treat on Margie's desk.

"Dun da dun dun," Herbie hummed again.

One by one they placed the treats on the desks. When they got to Annabelle's, she snapped, "Did you boys wash your hands before you made these?"

"We sure did," Ray said, placing a treat on Annabelle's desk.

The last one was given to the teacher.

"Thank you," Miss Pinkham said. "You may eat now, boys and girls."

Everyone bit into the Rice Krispies and crunched away.

Herbie couldn't eat his. He had to watch everyone else. Maybe he could stop them just in time if he had eagle eyes.

"Mmmmmm," Miss Pinkham said.

"Not bad," John said. "Of course, this doesn't compare to my Eskimo Pies."

Herbie had to force himself not to wish the purple treat on John.

"Quite good," Annabelle said. "The recipe is on the box?"

Ray licked his fingers as he eagerly told Annabelle the ingredients. "Right on the back. Just add margarine, marshmallows, and Rice Krispies."

"Really?"

Herbie started to peel off the cellophane from his treat. Maybe, he thought, just maybe Ray was right. Maybe his gum didn't fall into the bowl after all.

Miss Pinkham passed brown towels around for napkins.

"You didn't leave anything out?" Annabelle said.

"No," Ray said. "That's it."

"Then what's this chewy purple center?"

Herbie dropped his treat on his desk.

Ray's eyes bulged.

Both boys sang out, "DUN DA DUN DUN DUNNNN."

Annabelle's voice snarled, "Raymond Martin, it is not funny! Whatever this is, it doesn't belong in my treat!"

Ray covered his mouth. He didn't dare laugh.

"I know one thing for *sure*," Annabelle said. "I wouldn't be caught dead at your birthday party *now!*"

John just leaned back in his chair and snickered.

10
Birthday Blues

That day after school, the boys walked home together as usual. But this time, Ray didn't laugh or joke around. "I guess it's just you, me, and Jose going to my party."

"What about Margie and Sarah?"

"Annabelle told them about the purple goo. I think it grossed them out."

"Boy, I really goofed things up, Ray. I'm sorry."

"That's okay, Herbie. Annabelle wouldn't have come anyway. Maybe Margie and Sarah will change their minds."

As the boys got closer to the corner of Washington Avenue, they saw a gathering of people by the ice cream truck.

"All the ice cream is half price," Phillip called out.

"It's his last week before he starts his route again next spring," Margie added.

"I'M GETTING A BOMBER BAR!" John shouted.

Herbie reached into his pockets. "All right! One silver quarter. We can get a popsicle, Ray. What flavor do you want?"

Ray shrugged. "I don't care."

Now Herbie *knew* Ray had a bad case of the birthday blues. Ice cream didn't even cheer him up.

Just as Herbie was standing in line, John came over to Ray. "Don't get your hopes up about anyone leaving my party early."

Everyone turned and listened.

"I packed my loot bags last night and guess what? Each one has four goodies—including a bag of Lutz Potato Chips. No one will miss a thing by not going to your party."

Herbie felt like popping John one. What a rotten thing to do!

Ray walked up to Jose. "You're coming to my party, aren't you?"

Jose shrugged. "If I leave early, John said I won't get a loot bag."

Ray's eyes suddenly got watery. "I gotta go, Herbie," he said.

"Wait for me," Herbie replied. "I'm getting us a rainbow popsicle."

"I don't want anything," Ray cried. "I'm goin' home." Then he started to cross the street.

Herbie looked up. Someone on a bicycle wearing a helmet and leather jacket was speeding around the corner. "LOOK OUT, RAY!"

Ray was so blue about his birthday, he didn't hear Herbie, or see the bicycle. He just darted out behind the ice cream truck.

11
Ray!

That night, the Jones family sat around the phone and waited.

"What if it had been a car?" Mr. Jones said.

Mrs. Jones shook her head. "I've seen how you boys dash across the street sometimes. You don't always look both ways, and then double-check. It was a blessing that the man on the bicycle was okay."

Herbie tore a paper napkin into tiny pieces. "I can still see Ray flying up in the air when he got hit with that bike. And how *still* he lay on the street. When the ambulance came, his mother was crying, I was crying, *everyone* was crying. Even Annabelle and John." Herbie wiped his eyes with his shirt sleeve. He felt like he was going to start again.

Olivia petted Hamburger Head. "Ray is probably going to be fine, Herbie." She wanted to be optimistic for her brother's sake, but it was hard to hide her sad voice.

Herbie put his head down on the kitchen table. He didn't feel like saying anything more. He just wanted to pray for his buddy. Silently.

Grandpa Jones swept the floor. He wanted to keep busy.

Suddenly the phone rang.

And the dog barked.

For a moment, the Jones family just stared at the white wall phone. No one jumped to answer it.

Mrs. Jones did on the second ring. "H-Hello? Yes . . . uh-huh, uh-huh."

Everyone knew it was a call from the Martins and held their breath.

After a long minute of uh-huhs, Mrs. Jones finally said, "A concussion?"

Herbie immediately reached for the big blue dictionary on the refrigerator. Olivia helped him find the word.

"Uh-huh . . ."

" 'An injury of the head due to a violent jarring

and shock,'" Olivia whispered. "That's what I thought it was."

Herbie looked worried.

Then Mrs. Jones cupped the phone. "HE'S GOING TO BE OKAY! He just asked for a cheeseburger!"

Herbie threw his arms around his mother.

Olivia hugged her father.

Grandpa Jones started dancing around the kitchen with the broom handle.

"Well," Mrs. Jones said, "that's wonderful news, Mrs. Martin. We're so relieved." And then she hung up.

Herbie slapped his thigh and leaped high in the air. "YAHOOOOO!"

When he landed, he asked his mother a dozen questions.

"How is he?"

"How long is he going to be in the hospital?"

"Can I visit?"

Mrs. Jones sat down at the table. "It was a miracle. He got a concussion, but he's talking now. Thank the Lord."

Then she added, "He also got a big bruise."

"On his head?" Olivia asked.

"No. His rear end."

For the first time that night, everyone laughed. It was such a relief that Ray was okay.

"They're keeping him at the hospital tonight and tomorrow night for tests," Mrs. Jones said. "Then he'll go home Friday . . . if everything's okay."

"Can I visit?"

"Not at the hospital, Herbie. Mrs. Martin said he needs two days of quiet rest. You can visit him Saturday at his house."

"Saturday! What about his birthday party at the potato chip factory?"

"The trip's off, Herbie. Mrs. Martin asked that you tell everyone."

Herbie got a long face. "Boy, some birthday Ray's going to have this year."

12

Grandpa to the Rescue

That night Herbie couldn't sleep, so he turned on his light and started reading *Shane* again. When he heard footsteps walking across the attic and a knock on his door, he sat up. "Who is it?"

"Grandpa."

"Come on in!"

Grandpa Jones stepped inside the little room and sat down on the bed next to Herbie. "I saw your light on when I took your dad to work tonight, so I decided to stop by. Are you still worried about your buddy?"

"Yeah. What if one of those routine tests shows up something?"

"You know, Herbie, when your grandmother got sick two years ago and I had to wait around for the results of some test, I was a mess. I couldn't eat, sleep, or think about anything else but her. Then your dad gave me a bucket of paint and said to paint a chair. I moved that brush up and down and up and down. It helped just to do something simple, not think about anything but that brush goin' up and down."

Herbie leaned on his granddad. "See that chuck-wagon over there on the table? Ray and I painted it today. We were going to finish it after school. For Grandparents' Day tomorrow. But . . . we can't do it now."

"Why not? Ray would want it finished. It'll be something to do and a chance to get your mind on something else."

Herbie scooted out of bed and brought the shoe-box to his grandfather. The handkerchief was sagging inside.

"Nice wheels," Grandpa Jones said.

"Ray made those today in class."

"Neat pots and pans."

"I got those in the attic. They're Olivia's."

"Hmmm," Grandpa Jones hummed. "The handkerchief just needs some support."

"We couldn't figure out how to do that."

Grandpa Jones walked out into the attic. Herbie followed him. "This an old bin of clothes?"

"Yup."

Herbie watched his granddad sort through it. "Perfect."

Herbie's eyebrows shot up when he saw what his grandfather was dangling in midair.

Two bras.

"Do you have a pair of scissors?"

"Yeah," Herbie groaned, "but I'm *not* bringing those things to school."

"No one will know. Go get me the scissors."

Herbie walked back to his room and opened up a drawer. His dad was right about his grandpa. He was stubborn. There was no changing his mind.

Herbie watched his grandfather snip a few places in each bra and then pull out four wires, each in the shape of a horseshoe.

"Those wires were in . . . those things?"

Herbie didn't want to say the word "bra" out loud.

"You just learned one of women's many secrets,

Herbie. Now, let's tape these wires in the shoebox and drape that hanky over them."

Herbie started to chuckle. "Boy, will Ray be surprised when he finds out where the wiring came from."

Ten minutes later Herbie and his granddad finished taping the handkerchief inside the covered wagon.

"Gee, Grandpa, it looks great."

"And you look tired. Time to get back to bed now. We can play some poker tomorrow night."

"Poker? Really? I've never played."

"You haven't? Well, we'll take care of that."

Herbie scooted under the blankets. He felt a little better about things. "Are you coming to Grandparents' Day tomorrow?"

"Wouldn't miss it. That's why I drove your dad to work. I wanted to get used to your car since I'll be driving it to school tomorrow."

Then he kissed Herbie on the noggin. "Goodnight."

"Night, Pops."

13
Class Cards

Thursday morning, the class had a long conversation about Ray's accident. Miss Pinkham reviewed safety rules for crossing the street. And the class made get-well cards.

Annabelle showed hers to Herbie.

It was a picture of Ray in a hospital bed with vases of daisies on the window ledge. Ray was wearing flowered pajamas. On the inside were four rules:

Review These
Important Rules

1. Look both ways before you cross the street.

2. Cross in the crosswalk.

3. Don't jaywalk.

4. Even if the light says WALK, look both ways

Margie's card had a picture of a cemetery and a rainbow.

Inside she wrote:

I'm so happy you're not dead.

Herbie wrote a poem on his:

You're one tough cowboy
And my best friend.
I'm sorry you're laying in bed
I miss you already
You're one in a million.
But, next time use your head.

When John finished his card, he handed it to Herbie.

For Ray

Herbie read it. It was a picture of John's birthday party with one empty chair. John wrote:

I'm sorry you can't be at my birthday party. I'm sorry I can't be at yours. Next year, you can have your birthday on October 8. It's your turn.

Your Friend,
John

So John was finally compromising. But what did it mean now?

Birthdays, Herbie thought.

What kind of birthday was Ray going to have this year?

Herbie went over and told his friends that the potato chip party was off.

When everyone was finished making their cards, Miss Pinkham asked Herbie to drop them by Ray's house after school and then she added, "We're all so thankful Ray is going to be back on Monday. It was a miracle that he didn't break something. I know we'll *all* look twice now when we're crossing the street."

Annabelle nodded.

Herbie raised his hand. "Ray did have one small injury."

"What was that, Herbie?" Miss Pinkham asked.

"Bruised buns."

John and Phillip cracked up.

Annabelle flared her nostrils. "There is nothing funny about Ray's accident. He had a concussion."

Miss Pinkham nodded. "You're absolutely right, Annabelle."

Herbie knew they were right, but he still thought a bruised rear end was kind of funny.

14
Grandparents' Day

That afternoon, fifteen grandparents showed up for Grandparents' Day. They sat in the back of the room on folding chairs. Margie's grandmother videotaped all the presentations.

Annabelle was dressed in a long skirt like Susan B. Anthony, and she welcomed the visitors. She pointed out special things in her committee's dioramas.

Margie, who was Florence Nightingale, carried a first aid kit and bandaged Phillip's arm. She talked about how important it was to have clean bandages.

Sarah Sitwellington played Harriet Tubman and told how she helped the slaves escape in the Underground Railroad that wasn't really a railroad.

Herbie thought everything went smoothly until

Jose's lighting system for his lighthouse blew a fuse and the room turned dark.

After the lights came back on, and the other committees took a turn, it was Herbie's. He read the rules that the cow cooks had, held up his chuckwagon, and talked about the supplies on board.

"How did you get the covered part of the wagon to stay up?" John Greenweed asked.

"Special wiring," Herbie replied. Then he and his granddad exchanged smiles.

When Miss Pinkham chuckled, Herbie wondered if she knew.

Then he picked up *Shane*.

"My granddad first got me interested in the wild West with this book. I want to read you the beginning."

Grandpa Jones leaned forward and listened with the rest of the grandparents.

"He rode into our valley in the summer of '89. I was just a kid then, barely topping the backboard of father's old chuckwagon. I was on the upper rail of our small corral, soaking in the late afternoon sun, when I saw him far down the road where it swung into the valley from the open plain beyond.

"In that clear Wyoming air I could see him plainly, though he was still several miles away."

"Some people are special like Shane," Herbie said, and then he paused.

"Like Raymond Martin, who is in the hospital today. We were supposed to give this presentation together. I'm real thankful he's okay."

When everyone started clapping, Miss Pinkham stood up and thanked people for coming. She said it was the best Grandparents' Day she had ever had.

It wasn't the best day for Herbie. He missed Raymond and worried about him in the hospital.

As soon as the 3:00 bell rang, Herbie dashed for Ray's house. Mrs. Martin was just coming out the door when Herbie came running up the steps. He noticed she had fresh paint on her hand and cheek.

"Herbie!"

"Mrs. Martin! How's Ray?"

"He's doing fine. Sleeping mostly. I'm on my way to the hospital now, to be with him."

"Here are some cards from the class. Mine's on top."

Mrs. Martin smiled. "I'm glad you came by. I

wanted to talk to you about Ray's birthday Saturday."

"The potato chip party is still on?"

"No. But I have another idea."

Herbie listened as Mrs. Martin explained.

"That's wild! I'll tell all the kids. And my family, too. They can help."

"How nice, Herbie! Have your mother call me later tonight. Oh . . . and don't forget we want to keep this a secret from Ray."

"No problem, Mrs. Martin!"

"Ruf! Ruf!" Shadow barked.

"Shadow says he'll keep it a secret, too," Herbie said.

15
Ray's Surprise

Saturday, Ray lay on the living room couch. He was looking at his get-well cards for the sixth time.

"Did Herbie ask about me?"

"Of course he did."

Ray sat up. "Ouch!" His rear end was still sore. "I guess everyone's at John's birthday party. Probably at the batting cage now."

"Probably," Mrs. Martin said, adjusting the new painting of Raymond on the living room wall.

"Did Herbie say he was coming to visit me today?"

"He said he would."

When Mrs. Martin returned to the kitchen, Ray called his dog, who was sleeping in his favorite place. The doorway.

Shadow ambled over, jumped up on the couch, and plopped down on Ray's stomach. His paws were next to Ray's neck.

"Aren't you going to wish me happy birthday?" Ray said to his dog.

"RUF! RUF!"

"Thanks."

Ray looked over at the clock above the TV. It said 1:35. "Mom?"

Mrs. Martin stuck her head around the corner. "Yes?"

"Are you sure Herbie said he was dropping by?"

"He said he was dropping by."

"How come I can't go outside?"

"You can later today, dear."

Ray closed his eyes and took a catnap. When the clock chimed two, and there was a knock at the door, he woke up.

Mrs. Martin went to get it.

"Hi, Herbie."

"HERBIE!" Ray shouted, jumping off the couch.

The boys hugged each other.

"Hey, partner," Herbie said. "You look good."

"I *am* good."

"Happy Birthday, Ray."

"Thanks, Herbie. So, how was John's party?"

"Okay. I only hit two of the balls that came out of the pitching machine."

"Really? How many did John hit?"

"One less than Annabelle. Ten."

"How was the food?"

"Okay. My hot dog was burnt but I like it that way."

"Me, too. Did you put lots of mustard and relish on it?"

Herbie nodded. He knew Ray liked talking about food. "So, what do you want to do?"

Ray shrugged. He was a little disappointed Herbie didn't have a gift for him.

"Want to go outside in the backyard?" Herbie suggested.

"I don't know," Ray groaned. "I've been bugging Mom about going outside ever since I got home from the hospital. She always says later. I'll find out if later is now. MOM! CAN I GO OUTSIDE?"

"Fine, dear."

"YEAH! We're out of here!" Ray said, bolting for the back door.

When he opened it up, he was shocked.

"SURPRISE!"

Ray looked at all the familiar faces and the wild West scene that was created in his own backyard. Margie was sitting in a big wheelbarrow of hay. Phillip and John poked their faces outside a big picture board of a covered wagon and two drivers. One was a cowboy and the other was a woman in a bonnet.

Ray laughed when he saw Phillip's face under the bonnet. "You painted that, Mom!" Ray exclaimed.

Mrs. Martin nodded.

Jose was playing poker at a card table with Herbie's granddad. "Come into the saloon and have some root beer!" Grandpa Jones called.

Ray slapped his thigh.

Annabelle was lassoing Ray's old childhood rocking horse. "I've done it once. Now I'm trying a second time."

"YAHOO!" Ray shouted.

Sarah held up a piece of aluminum foil that was

shaped like a star. "Want to play pin the badge on the sheriff?"

"Mom! You painted that six-foot sheriff on the cardboard, too?"

"I like to paint."

"Wow!" Ray said. "I never thought about a wild West party. That's even better than touring a potato chip factory."

"So, what do you want to play first?" Mr. Martin said, wheeling the wheelbarrow across the backyard. Everyone could tell Margie loved the ride. She was tossing hay in the air and giggling the whole time.

Ray looked around. It was a tough decision. Everything looked like so much fun. "Well, why don't we start here," he said, pointing to a blanket in front of him that was piled high with boxes.

"THE PRESENTS!" everyone shouted.

Herbie nodded. "I knew it. Come on! Let's all sit down and watch."

Ray corrected his buddy. "I'll stand this year."

Phillip cracked up. "You gotta open mine first. It's just what you need. Here."

PAN for GOLD

HAPPY BIRT

Ray did. "A whoopie cushion! Neato!" Then he sat down on it.

Mrs. Martin rolled her eyes when it made funny pooping noises.

"Thanks, Phil. I guess you knew about my bruised buns."

"Everyone did," Phillip replied, cackling some more. He loved silly sounds.

Then Raymond reached for the second present. "Man, this is a big one!"

Annabelle beamed. "It's also educational. Not dumb like the one Herbie gave me last year."

Everyone laughed. They remembered Herbie's can of salmon.

Ray ripped the flowered wrapping paper. "Wow! Neato! A Frog Hatchery Kit."

"You mail the coupon inside and they send you the frog eggs."

"Thanks, Annabelle."

"Eh . . . there's something else inside that little envelope," Annabelle said.

Ray opened it. Then his eyes bulged.

"Grape gum?"

Herbie and Ray exchanged looks. So she knew, they both thought.

Annabelle just snickered.

As Ray opened the rest of the presents, he saved Herbie's for last. It wasn't very big and it wasn't very heavy. Ray unwrapped the aluminum foil and smiled.

"*Shane!*" Then he read the inside inscription aloud:

For my partner Ray
 on his 9th birthday,
  when you ride into town,
   Make sure you look both ways.
     Your buddy,
       Herbie

"I will. TWICE!" Ray exclaimed.

And everyone clapped.

"Now, let's party!" Phillip said, running over to the empty chairs at the poker game. "Deal me in."

"YEEHAW!" Herbie shrieked, twirling the lasso toward Shadow.

"I'm panning for gold!" John said as he took a pie plate from Olivia and scooped it in a plastic pool of sand and water. When he came up with two copper pennies, Annabelle got next in line.

"CHOW TIME!" Ray called and he raced to the food table. "I want to munch on a wagon wheel."

"Coming up!" Mrs. Jones replied, handing him a fresh donut that dripped with sugary glaze.

An hour later, when John had won a bag of 57 M&M's at the poker table—playing seven-card stud and spit in the ocean—he strolled over to Ray.

Herbie stepped out of the wheelbarrow and joined them.

"Some party, Ray!" John said. "What do you say we shake hands and promise *never* to have another birthday showdown again?"

"I can't," Ray said.

"You can't. Why not?"

"My hands are full of chicken nuggets."

John and Herbie cracked up. "Okay. We'll just take each other's word for it. Right, Ray?"

"Right, John."

And that was when Herbie tossed some hay in the air, threw his arms around his two friends, and shouted, "YEEHAW!"

DUE /DATE

APR 1994